A VERY SPECIAL KWANZAA

Other Little Apple paperbacks
you might enjoy:

Good Grief . . . Third Grade
by Colleen O'Shaughnessy McKenna

Striped Ice Cream
by Joan M. Lexau

Class Clown
by Johanna Hurwitz

A VERY SPECIAL KWANZAA

Debbi Chocolate

A
LITTLE APPLE
PAPERBACK

SCHOLASTIC INC.
New York Toronto London Auckland Sydney

No part of this publication may be reproduced in whole or in part, or stored in a retrieval system, or transmitted in any form or by any means, electronic, mechanical, photocopying, recording, or otherwise, without written permission of the publisher. For information regarding permission, write to Scholastic Inc., 555 Broadway, New York, NY 10012.

ISBN 0-590-84862-3

12 11 10 9 8 7   1/0

Printed in the U.S.A.   40

First Scholastic printing, November 1996

For Steve, the best brother ever.

1

Ms. Marmelsteen was busy decorating the icy windows in her classroom with Christmas drawings. Just as she looked down on the school yard the morning bell rang. Her fourth-graders began filing noisily into the building and up the stairs, along with the other school children. When they reached the cloakroom, her charges did what fourth-graders dressed for cold weather do in classrooms everywhere: haphazardly threw off their mufflers, winter jackets, and rubber boots.

Chirping like tiny sparrows, their conversations turned to Christmas and to the gifts they were expecting. The boys boasted about the train sets and racing cars they would find beneath their trees on Christmas morning. The girls chatted about the dolls and roller skates that topped their Christmas wish lists. Ms. Marmelsteen, who had taught the same children in third grade, was delighted to have been asked by Mr. O'Malley, the principal, to teach them as fourth-graders, after Mr. Bailey retired.

Ms. Marmelsteen treated the fourth-graders as though they were her very own. She adored every one of them. "Good morning, class," interrupted Ms. Marmelsteen in her familiar syrupy-sweet voice.

"Good morn-ing, Miz Mar-mel-steen," sang the fourth grade in unison.

"Now, children, you mustn't dawdle this morning. Quickly! Get to your seats," she gently but firmly prodded them. Ms. Marmelsteen had an important announcement to make.

After the Pledge of Allegiance, Ms. Marmelsteen wrote the words *Kwanzaa Festival* in big loopy letters all the way across the blackboard. Charlie Potter stared at the blackboard and let out a long miserable groan. Charlie sat at a desk near the windows and Christmas decorations. His best friend, Louie Rodriguez, sat beside him. When Louie heard Charlie groan he leaned over and whispered, "Hey, Charlie, what's the matter? Why are you all of a sudden looking so sick?"

Charlie didn't answer his best friend. He just sat there, his coffee-brown-colored face frozen in a bleak stare. As he stared at the words, *Kwanzaa Festival*, images began flooding his mind. Images of last year's Kwanzaa celebration.

What a disaster that had been.

Last year, Ms. Marmelsteen had been delighted when she found out that Charlie's

father owned a shop in the westside neighborhood where they lived. Charlie's dad sold African clothing and jewelry. At the Kwanzaa Festival, while Ms. Marmelsteen put on a slide show of the African continent, Charlie had to stand in front of the whole class dressed in beads, a *dashiki*, and sandals. Sandals! In the middle of winter! With his hammer toe sticking out! That was the worst part. Everyone could see Charlie's hideous toe, which was balled up into a claw with a knot of hard, dry skin on top.

Halfway through the presentation, Ms. Marmelsteen had been called into the principal's office. That was when Gilbert Crenshaw, the meanest, sneakiest boy in the whole third grade, had shown up late to class as usual.

"Eeee-ew, gross!" Gilbert had blurted out. "Charlie! Your toe looks like a gargoyle's toe." The classroom had exploded in laughter. Charlie had never been so embarrassed in his life.

By the second week of third grade

Charlie had discovered that "sneaky" and "mean" were the best words ever to describe Gilbert. Whenever Ms. Marmelsteen called anyone to the blackboard, Gilbert stuck his size nine tennis shoes in the aisle and sent the kid hurtling at the speed of light. After which Gilbert would always smirk, "Have a nice trip, moron, see you in the fall."

Not only was Gilbert Crenshaw mean, he was also the biggest thief Charlie had ever laid eyes on. Gilbert stole pencils, erasers, and notebook paper from other kids' desks. Gilbert stole sandwiches from other kids' lunch boxes. And if somebody's mother put a napkin in his lunch box so he could wipe the crumbs from his mouth, Gilbert stole that, too.

So last year, as soon as Ms. Marmelsteen disappeared into the principal's office, Gilbert ran to the front of the class, where he grabbed a *kaba* blouse and an African skirt from Ms. Marmelsteen's desk. Quickly he slipped the costume over his T-shirt and jeans. Then Gilbert stood on top of Ms. Marmelsteen's desk and did a hula dance. Everybody laughed like crazy. Everybody except for Charlie and Louie, that is. Even Louie was dying to laugh. The only reason he held it in was because Charlie was his best friend.

Later that day, Ms. Marmelsteen stood in front of the class pronouncing the names of the African clothes in Swahili. "Now class, does any one of you remember the Swahili word for this little gem?" She held up a rainbow-colored handwoven hat. It had once belonged to Charlie's grandfather. Gilbert had practically done flips in the aisle to get Ms. Marmelsteen's attention.

"All right, Gilbert," said Ms. Marmelsteen. "Which Swahili word do we use to describe this *bee-yoo-ti-ful* hat?"

Instead of saying *koo-fy,* the way it was supposed to be pronounced, Gilbert shouted: "I know! It's a *goofy!*" And once again, along with Gilbert, the whole class screamed with laughter.

When Ms. Marmelsteen spread a bright, boldly colored African cloth on her desk and explained that it was *kente* cloth once worn by African kings and queens in Ghana, Gilbert made a wisecrack.

"So what does that make Charlie when he wears *kente*? A prince or a princess?" Ms. Marmelsteen had made Gilbert stand out in the hall for that. But that hadn't changed the way Charlie felt. He felt like totally disappearing.

At lunchtime, Gilbert had hung around the cafeteria pointing out how funny Charlie's toes looked in sandals. Charlie didn't think his toes looked funny at all. Well, maybe the hammer toe he inherited from his aunt Velma did look a *little* weird.

"And now, Charlie," sang Ms. Marmelsteen, bringing Charlie back to the present. "Would you care to tell the class what Kwanzaa teaches us?"

Charlie sat up in his seat. Reluctantly, he let the words, "Kwanzaa teaches people how to live together," squeeze past his lips.

"And what else?" Ms. Marmelsteen said cheerfully, prompting him along.

"It teaches us how to work together," Charlie pouted.

"That's right," said Ms. Marmelsteen, pleased. "Now, class — I'm sure some of you remember how delightful our third-grade celebration was last year. Well, this year's celebration promises to be a very, very special one indeed. Our class has been invited to organize Doolittle School's first school-wide Kwanzaa ever." Ms. Marmelsteen's eyelashes fluttered as she clasped her hands together beneath her chin and beamed.

"Cripes," moaned Charlie under his breath. Then he wriggled so low in his chair he was practically sitting underneath his desk.

"Now does anyone of you remember anything at all about the Kwanzaa season?"

"I remember something about Kwanzaa, Ms. Marmelsteen," yelled Louie, waving his hand frantically in the air.

"Good, Louie," smiled Ms. Marmelsteen.

"I remember it starts the day after Christmas," he said. "And people give gifts. Sort of like the three wise guys did for the baby Jesus at the first Christmas." Everybody laughed.

"Wise *men*, Louie, not wise guys," corrected Ms. Marmelsteen. Hidden beneath his desk, even Charlie had to laugh. Sometimes Louie could really be funny.

"But it *is* something like that, Louie," smiled Ms. Marmelsteen. "Kwanzaa *is* a little like Christmas. Except that Kwanzaa isn't a religious holiday like Christmas is," she explained. "And the gifts of Kwanzaa are usually handmade."

Sarah Goldman raised her hand. "Kwanzaa is a little like Christmas, and a little like Thanksgiving and Hanukkah all rolled up into one," she said.

"That's right, Sarah," Ms. Marmelsteen acknowledged. "Can you tell us some more about that?"

"Well, Kwanzaa's a little like Christmas

because of the sharing of gifts. And it's a little like Thanksgiving because of all the feasting that takes place. And it's a little like Hanukkah because, well — when my family celebrates Hanukkah every year at my Uncle Shelley's house, we light candles each day just like they do at Kwanzaa season."

"Well done," beamed Ms. Marmelsteen. "It's really quite an honor to have our class invited to prepare a school-wide festival, children. But we have a thousand and one things to do, and only one week to do them in. As you all know from last year, Mr. Potter, Charlie's father, owns a shop and sells African clothes and jewelry. Mr. Potter has volunteered again this year to bring in clothes and jewelry and other things to sell."

Ms. Marmelsteen turned around to face the blackboard. Then in big loopy letters, underneath the words, *Kwanzaa Festival*, she scribbled the words: *This Friday! — December 19th!*

By now Charlie was feeling absolutely miserable. As the drone of Ms. Marmelsteen's voice floated in and out of his ears, Charlie's thoughts drifted to last year's Kwanzaa celebration and the disaster that this year's festival promised to bring him.

He tried to shut out the sound of Ms. Marmelsteen's voice. But he could still hear her. Reaching blindly inside his desk he grabbed a geography book. He opened the book and used it to cover his ears. But it didn't help.

At the desk beside Charlie, Louie was stretching his neck trying to catch a glimpse of Charlie's face. But he was barely able to see the top of Charlie's head.

On the other side of the room was Gilbert Crenshaw. Whenever Ms. Marmelsteen turned her back, Gilbert jumped up from his chair and made weird faces at Charlie while all the other children struggled hard not to laugh. When Ms. Marmelsteen turned to face the class, Gilbert was sitting like a perfect angel with his hands folded on his desk.

Then something weird happened. Right before lunch Ms. Marmelsteen returned to the blackboard. That's when Gilbert jumped up. He hopped on top of his chair and did a wild jig and a crazy hula dance, making everybody scream with laughter.

2

Even before he opened the door to his family's apartment, Charlie could smell potatoes and onions frying, and a roast baking in the oven. His sister, Tamika, was sitting at the dining room table, surrounded by a sea of red poinsettias, cutting up narrow strips of colored construction paper. Tamika was in the sixth grade at Doolittle. She was a whole foot taller than Charlie, but they both looked just like their father.

"Come here for a minute," said Tamika when she heard Charlie come in. "Tell me if you like these colors." Tamika spread the strips of papers into a rainbow-colored fan on the dining room table. There were strips of violet and gold, red and green, blue and orange, and black. Charlie looked over his sister's shoulder.

"I'm weaving a mat for our Kwanzaa Festival at school," Tamika explained.

Charlie groaned.

"Don't you like the colors?" asked Tamika.

"Tamika, Kwanzaa colors are red, black, and green," he sighed, flopping down on the couch, his book bag still on his back.

"*I* know that," said Tamika, putting her hands on her hips. "I'm trying to be creative. Don't you remember *kuumba*? The Kwanzaa principle that stands for creativity. I'm trying to do something different this year."

"Yeah, me too," mumbled Charlie.

"Yoo-hoo . . . *Chaaaarleee*? Is that you, honey?" Ms. Potter's voice rang out from the kitchen.

"It's me, Mama," Charlie yelled back. Ms. Potter followed her son's voice into the living room. She had cake flour on her forehead and was wiping flour from her hands onto her apron.

"Guess who called today? Ms. Marmelsteen," said Charlie's mother. Ms. Potter was all smiles. From the look on her face, thought Charlie, you would've thought it was Christmas Eve or the sixth day of Kwanzaa. Charlie groaned again.

"Ms. Marmelsteen says the fourth-grade class is planning a Kwanzaa Festival for the entire school and she's asked me to help. Your dad's going to set up a booth and sell some things from the shop and — "

"Maybe we should use a little more creativity this year," Charlie blurted out. "You know, a little more *kuumba*." Tamika narrowed her eyes at her brother. Ignoring his sister, Charlie said excitedly, "Yeah! Maybe we could even celebrate a different holiday."

"A different holiday?" Ms. Potter sounded puzzled.

Charlie fell silent. Then suddenly his eyes brightened. "Something like *Feliz Navidad*. The way Louie and his family do every year."

Ms. Potter put her hands on her hips and smiled. "Charlie," she explained, "*Feliz Navidad* is Spanish for Merry Christmas."

"Well how about Hanukkah then?"

"Hanukkah?" laughed Ms. Potter. "Charlie Potter, what's gotten into you? The school celebrated Hanukkah last year. Besides," she explained, "Doolittle School never celebrated Kwanzaa before. The way Ms. Marmelsteen explained it, she's trying to share the spirit of Kwanzaa with the whole school this year, instead of with just one class."

"Mama," said Tamika excitedly, "I think I smell your roast burning." Ms. Potter dropped her argument and dashed off to the kitchen to save her supper.

That night over supper the Potters talked excitedly about the Doolittle Kwanzaa Festival: What would they cook? Which *dashikis* and *lappas* would they wear? Mr. Potter had a new shipment in of African shirts, *kente* cloth, and cowry shells. Everyone was talking at once. Everyone except Charlie, that is. He pretended he wasn't feeling well and asked to be excused from the table.

Once inside his room Charlie felt his face slowly turning hot. Warm tears welled up in his eyes, then splashed onto his cheeks. He picked up his plastic penny jug and hugged it close to his chest. From his windowseat, he stared at the newfallen snow just outside his window.

He found himself thinking about the coming Kwanzaa Festival and about Gilbert Crenshaw. Charlie didn't want to be the laughingstock of his class again. But what could he do to stop Gilbert from making things so miserable for him? How could he stop Gilbert from making fun of his Af-

rican clothes? Or calling him a princess? Or laughing at his hammer toe in front of all the other kids? Tears were still streaming down his face when Charlie heard a knock on his bedroom door. He jumped up and ran to his bed where he grabbed a pillow to bury his face in. Charlie heard the bedroom door open. The voice that followed belonged to Mr. Potter.

"Is it all right if I come in, champ?" Charlie didn't answer. He kept his face buried in the pillow because he didn't want his father to know he had been crying.

Mr. Potter sat down on the bed next to Charlie. He picked up the caboose and a couple of freight cars that belonged to Charlie's miniature electric train set. He filled the silence between him and Charlie by toying with the metal wheels of the cars, trying to get them to spin. But the wheels would not spin because they were all broken. After awhile Mr. Potter set the train cars back on the track.

"What's the matter, son?" began Mr. Potter, leaning back on the bed. "You used to have so much fun at Kwanzaa time. You used to love celebrating the *karamu* feast and watching the candles being lit."

"I still do," admitted Charlie. It wasn't Kwanzaa that Charlie didn't like. He loved celebrating Kwanzaa at home, where family and friends gathered. It was celebrating Kwanzaa at school, where Gilbert made fun of him in front of the other kids that bothered Charlie so much.

"You used to really enjoy Kwanzaa," his father reminisced. "Remember that rocking horse Grandpa made for you two years ago for a Kwanzaa gift?" Charlie wiped the tears from his eyes with his pillow. Now he looked at his father and frowned. Of course he remembered. Grandpa had made the rocking horse when Charlie was in second grade. What his father didn't know was that even though Charlie had outgrown the rocking horse, every now and then he still stole a ride on it down in the basement of the apartment building. *Remember?* How

21

could Charlie ever forget when it was only the best Kwanzaa gift he had ever gotten.

"Your mama and I have been thinking," said Mr. Potter. "Maybe this year you could help light the candles for the *karamu* feast." Charlie's eyes lit up. For as long as he could remember he had been waiting to help light the Kwanzaa candles. Tamika had been lighting candles since she was in third grade.

"And on the last night of Kwanzaa," his father went on, "I thought we could both wear matching *dashikis*." Charlie smiled and wiped his nose with the back of his hand. He looked thoughtfully up at his father. "I thought maybe we could dress alike for the school festival, too. You could help me sell things from the booth." Suddenly the light went out of Charlie's eyes just as quickly as it had appeared. The light was replaced with a look of despair.

"What's the matter, champ?" asked Mr. Potter. All was quiet. Then, reluctantly,

Charlie began to tell his father about Gilbert Crenshaw.

"It's some of the guys at school," he began. "Some of them think Kwanzaa is pretty dumb."

"Dumb?" said Mr. Potter, surprised. He sat up on the bed.

Charlie hung his head. He tried to explain as best he could. "Last year," he said, "Gilbert Crenshaw made fun of my African clothes." Mr. Potter sighed.

"Gilbert called my *kufi* a goofy, instead of a crown," said Charlie. Then it was Mr. Potter's turn to frown.

"Well," said his father, "that *is* pretty awful." Charlie thought it was awful, too. He was glad his father understood. Maybe it meant he wouldn't have to be in the Kwanzaa Festival after all.

"Maybe Gilbert's problem is that he doesn't understand what Kwanzaa's all about," said Mr. Potter. "Maybe we can help him understand by putting together the best Kwanzaa ever at school."

Charlie looked at his father out of the corner of his eye. His father hadn't understood at all. Charlie didn't want to celebrate Kwanzaa at school this year. Even if it meant he'd have to give up lighting the Kwanzaa candles at home with family and friends.

"I don't think so, Dad," said Charlie, wiping his nose again. "Gilbert Crenshaw's a real *jerk*. He doesn't care about Kwanzaa, or about finding out what Kwanzaa's all about."

"Well, maybe we can change that," insisted Mr. Potter. "Tell you what," he said in a serious tone. "Why don't we just try ignoring Gilbert. When he says something to make fun of you, don't pay him any attention. Sometimes," said Mr. Potter, "ignoring people like Gilbert makes them go away." He paused for a moment. And then he said, "What do you say, son?"

Sullenly, Charlie looked up at his father

and answered. "Yeah, okay, Dad. Whatever you say."

Mr. Potter stood up. He squeezed Charlie's shoulder and left the room. Charlie reached over and played with the broken wheels on his train set. He counted the pennies in his penny jug. He hadn't agreed with what his father had said. But he couldn't seem to get his father's words out of his head. "Sometimes ignoring people like Gilbert makes them go away."

"Shuh right!" said Charlie to himself. Gilbert Crenshaw wasn't *people*, he thought. Gilbert Crenshaw was a *bully*. And Charlie knew that Gilbert was not the kind of bully you could make "go away" simply by ignoring him.

3

Nearly half the next morning had been spent in classroom dress rehearsals, then, later, decorating the gym for the Kwanzaa Festival. Ms. Marmelsteen chose Charlie, in his traditional African clothing, to light the candles, Louie to work the slide projector, and Gilbert to greet parents and guests at the gymnasium door. When they finally got back to class Ms. Marmelsteen announced:

"Class, your weekly writing assignment is a holiday composition about the one special gift you've decided to give this year." The class groaned in unison. "You may write about a special Christmas gift, Kwanzaa gift, or a Hanukkah gift. All compositions are due on Friday." Louie Rodriguez shot his hand into the air.

"Ms. Marmelsteen," he said, "can I do a composition on what *Feliz Navidad* means to me?"

"Of course, Louie," Ms. Marmelsteen smiled patiently, "but remember to mention something about your special gift. For those of you who don't remember from our Christmas Around the World project, *Feliz Navidad* means — "

"Merry Christmas in Spanish!" Gilbert blurted out.

"Estupido!" yelled Louie. "We all know that." Calling Gilbert stupid made everybody laugh.

"Gilbert!" scolded Ms. Marmelsteen, "it's rude to interrupt when others are speaking. Louie! Mind your language," she spoke sharply. "Now class," she continued, "those of you who have not finished your art projects for the Kwanzaa Festival please work on them now and bring them to class on Friday along with your compositions."

Charlie and Louie met in the back of the room at the art supply cabinet where other students were busy gathering huge pieces of construction paper, metallic paper, glitter, colored yarn, scissors, glue, and Styrofoam.

"Hey," said Charlie, searching for scissors in the supply drawer, "all the scissors are gone."

"Mine are in my coat pocket," offered Louie. "Why don't you go take a look."

Inside the cloakroom Charlie hunted for Louie's coat. He finally found it hanging on a hook next to Billy Jamison's new Starter jacket. As Charlie searched the pockets for the pair of scissors, he noticed for the first time that Louie's winter coat wasn't really much of a coat at all. It was more like a baseball jacket. The kind that kids on Little League teams usually wore in summer.

Thin and worn, there were patches sewn on the sleeves of both elbows. And on the back of the jacket the team logo had been completely washed off.

As he fumbled with the jacket Charlie discovered one pocket was torn and that the other had a hole clean through it. There weren't any scissors anywhere to be found. But something on the floor glinted in the pool of light streaming down from the window. Charlie knelt to pick it up and was surprised to find the glint of light came from Louie's scissors. He straightened Louie's jacket on the cloakroom hook and a cold shiver went through him. The thought of Louie wearing a thin baseball jacket all winter suddenly made Charlie feel cold. He crossed back into the classroom, sat down on the floor beside his friend, and handed Louie the scissors.

"Who are you going to give that one special gift to this year, Louie?" Charlie teased, mimicking Ms. Marmelsteen. The boys looked at each other with crooked smiles and couldn't help but laugh out loud.

"I don't know," admitted Louie, sounding serious. "To tell you the truth, I haven't even started to think about it. My pop's been out of work since Thanksgiving. I wanted to give him something special this year. But, there's no money."

At first Charlie didn't say anything. And then he said, "You could make your father a Kwanzaa gift. That's what Kwanzaa's all about. You're really not supposed to *buy* gifts at Kwanzaa time. Kwanzaa gifts are special because it's something you make with your own hands and with your own mind."

"I don't know," said Louie doubtfully. "I'm not good at making things."

"I could help you," offered Charlie.

"You would?" said Louie excitedly. "Then let's get started."

The two boys gathered art supplies, then sat together near the Scotch pine Christmas tree at the window. It was still snowing outside. The drifting snow and the piney scent of the tree began to warm Charlie with the holiday spirit. After playing around with the art supplies for awhile, Louie decided he wanted to make a *piñata* for his father. He would fill the *piñata* with family photographs and Christmas candy and nuts and tangerines, from the penny candy store. And it wouldn't cost too much. He could earn money by running errands after school for people in the neighborhood.

Louie needed a big round flowerpot to shape his *piñata*. So he asked Ms. Marmelsteen if he could use the empty pot by the fishbowl. He told Charlie that the pot was as big and round as his Uncle Tito's belly.

Louie made a handle for the *piñata* by tying twine around the neck of the pot. He and Charlie glued sheets of old newspapers around the ceramic belly. Afterwards Charlie found some cardboard. He drew narrow dragon eyes, ears, feet, a long tail, and a very, very long tongue and neck, and finally some ferocious-looking fangs. Then

31

together he and Louie cut the dragon parts out and carefully pasted them onto the pot. While they waited for the glue to dry, Louie gathered colored tissue paper — red, orange, blue and green, gold, black and white. Then he and Charlie cut the tissue into strips. Row after row, they pasted the bright tissue paper colors on.

Louie decided to use red metallic paper for the eyes and for the tongue to make them glitter. Finally, they took out paint jars and paintbrushes. Louie painted the ears and fangs yellow. Charlie painted the feet and tail a bright orange.

Ms. Marmelsteen took out her cassette player and played Christmas songs for the class. When "The Twelve Days of Christmas" came on, Charlie found himself humming along.

While everyone was busy working on their projects, Ms. Marmelsteen sat working at the computer. It was beginning to get warm in the room and every now and then Ms. Marmelsteen fanned herself with a thin paperback book.

"Hey, Louie," said Charlie, elbowing his friend. "Look at Ms. Marmelsteen. She doesn't look too good." Louie looked hard at Ms. Marmelsteen. To Louie, she looked like she always did. Plump and rosy and happy-looking. As though absolutely nothing in the world could make her cross or mean.

"She always looks weird like that," said Louie, picking up the scissors to cut more strips of tissue paper.

"No. Really. Look at her," insisted Charlie. "Doesn't she look a little pale?" As both boys stared at Ms. Marmelsteen Charlie's eyes grew wider and wider. Suddenly, with excitement in his voice he said, "Hey! Maybe she's coming down with the flu or something. Maybe by Friday she'll be so sick she won't be able to come to school. Or maybe her computer is infecting her with some unknown virus. Maybe Ms. Marmelsteen will end up floating helplessly out in cyberspace some place where no one can find her. And then maybe, just maybe — there won't even be a Kwanzaa Festival!"

"Man, Charlie!" said Louie. "Where do you get this stuff?"

Charlie sighed hopelessly. "From television?"

Turning back to his *piñata* Louie said, "Anyway, thanks for getting me started." Then carefully, Louie glued more metallic paper onto the cardboard fangs. "My pops will really be surprised," he said.

As they worked on putting the finishing touches on Louie's *piñata*, Charlie began to think about Tamika and the rainbow-colored mat she was making. He looked around the room. Everyone else was working. Getting into the holiday spirit. Even Louie, who really hadn't much of anything to give except old photographs and penny candy. Charlie looked at the snowflakes falling outside the window. He thought about Gilbert and how Gilbert was taking all the fun out of Kwanzaa for him. When he looked back at Louie he saw that his friend was concentrating very hard on gluing the wings onto the *piñata*, which was beginning to look more and more like a real dragon. As he watched Louie work, Charlie began to think about his own project and about the special gift he might give.

"Hey, Charlie," said Louie all of a sudden. "Who are you going to give your special gift to?"

"I don't know," Charlie answered.

"I know!" said Louie excitedly. "You and your dad are really good at woodcarving. Why don't you carve something special for the Kwanzaa Festival?"

"I never carved anything by myself before," shrugged Charlie.

"So what," said Louie. "Just because you never did it before doesn't mean you can't. Look at me. I never made a *piñata* before. But this is beginning to look okay. Don't you think so?" Louie held up his *piñata*. Charlie studied the brightly colored dragon then nodded his head in agreement with his friend.

"Yeah. That does look pretty cool," he said. Maybe Louie was right. Maybe he *could* carve something for the Kwanzaa Festival. But what?

Suddenly it came to him.

"The *kinara*!" cried Charlie excitedly.

"The what?"

"The *kinara*. The wooden candle holder my dad and I have been working on," explained Charlie. "We've been making Kwanzaa gifts for everyone. Maybe I could finish the *kinara* by myself."

"I think you could. After all," said Louie, "you're the best woodcarver in the whole fourth grade."

While he helped Louie clean up for lunch, all Charlie could think about was putting the finishing touches on the *kinara*. By the time the lunch bell rang, Charlie had made up his mind. He would go by Mr. Jackson's hardware store on the way home and pick up a can of shellac. After dinner he would finish carving the candle holder, even if it took all night. Then when it was done, he would paint the shellac onto the *kinara* and make it shine like glass for the holiday of lights.

4

The next day at lunchtime, following final dress rehearsals, the chalkboard menu in the school cafeteria read:

> Foot-Long Hot Dog
>   on a Bun
> French Fries
> Baked Beans
> Orange Slushy
>
> Soft Shell
>   Beef Taco

Spanish Rice
Mexicorn
Grapes

Grilled Cheese
  Sandwich
Tomato Soup
Tater Tots
Pickle Wedges

After standing in the long lunch line for what seemed like forever, listening to their stomachs growl, Charlie and Louie finally reached the cafeteria steam tables. Charlie was so hungry that he didn't realize he was still in sandals and that his *kufi* was still on his head. He ordered the beef taco lunch and Louie ordered the foot-long hot dog with french fries. As soon as they sat down to eat Gilbert appeared.

"Hey, Loonie!" he teased Louie. "Lemme have some fries." Stuffing his mouth with the foot-long hot dog Louie shook his head in protest, but that didn't stop Gilbert from snatching a handful of fries off his plate. Charlie jumped up. This was the last straw.

"Why don't you go somewhere else?" he shouted at Gilbert over the noisy cafeteria.

"Who's gonna make me?" snarled Gilbert, snatching another handful of fries. Then, suddenly, without warning, Gilbert snatched Charlie's hat, dashed out of the cafeteria, and headed for the playground. Following close behind, Charlie and Louie grabbed their jackets and chased after him.

Outside the snow was coming down even heavier than it had in the morning. In the center of the playground the younger kids were lying in the snow making snow angels while the older kids busied themselves playing "pop the whip" on the smooth, thick sheet of ice covering the blacktop. There were snow mounds, slippery from the forming ice, near Ms. Lee's sixth-grade classroom window, where some of the children tugged at each other in the climb up to become king of the hill.

"Aren't your feet cold?" Louie asked.

Charlie looked down and saw that he still had on his sandals.

"Only a little," he lied. He looked around the school yard for Gilbert.

"It doesn't matter," said Louie, "the bell's getting ready to ring." Charlie thought it would be okay as long as he didn't try to climb the snow mounds or let his feet get too wet. But he was determined to catch up with Gilbert and get his *kufi* back. Suddenly, out of nowhere, someone tackled him from behind. Charlie fell hard. When he looked up, Gilbert was standing over him, wearing his hat. Another school bully, Marcus Johnson, was stringing along behind.

"Hey! African princess!" teased Marcus, snatching Charlie's crown from Gilbert's head and putting it on. Charlie tried to stand up but it was hard to regain his balance in sandals. Instead, he slipped and slid on the icy blacktop. But even sprawled on the ground Charlie shouted at the two bullies.

"Hey! Give it back!" he demanded. Marcus tossed the rainbow-colored hat to Gilbert. Soaring high through the drifting snow, Charlie's crown looked more like a flying Frisbee than a handwoven *kufi*.

"Come and get it," taunted Gilbert. Then he and Marcus climbed the two biggest snow mounds in the whole school yard. From the top of the mounds the two bullies tossed Charlie's *kufi* back and forth. Charlie glanced down at his feet, which were really beginning to get cold now. He didn't stand a chance of climbing the icy mounds in sandals and Gilbert and Marcus knew it. But that was the only way he was going to get his hat back. Charlie glanced over his shoulder at Louie.

"Wait here," said Louie. "I'll get Ms. Marmelsteen." Before Charlie could say anything, Louie was running off toward the door leading to the cafeteria.

"Yo, princess!" yelled Gilbert from atop the mound. "Where'd your pal Loonie go?"

"I'll bet he went to squeal like a rat to Ms. Marmelsteen," Marcus guessed.

"I don't need any teacher to make you give me back my hat," shouted Charlie.

"Well then climb up the hill and get it yourself, pinhead," said Gilbert.

Then, without giving it another thought, Charlie dug his fingers into the mound of icy snow where Gilbert stood king. Using both his hands and his feet, Charlie climbed slowly, taking a step at a time. But his feet were beginning to ache from the cold. And what was worse, he didn't have his gloves. He had left them at home warming on the radiator in his room this morning. On his first try, Charlie slid swiftly right back down to the foot of the mound. Gilbert and Marcus laughed until tears rolled from their eyes.

"C'mon," teased Marcus, "you can do better than that."

"Yeah, c'mon onion breath," Gilbert pressured, "give it the old army try."

Charlie got up and brushed the snow from his jacket. Snow was packed between his toes from the climb and his feet were beginning to feel numb now. He glanced back at the door leading to the cafeteria. There was no sight of Louie or Ms. Marmelsteen. So turning his attention back to the two bullies, Charlie quickly sized up the snow on Marcus's mound. The snow looked softer there so he decided to try climbing it instead.

"C'mon, dirtwad," taunted Marcus. "What's there to think about?"

As Charlie dug into Marcus's snowhill he could feel the ice give. The snow *was* softer here and it would be easier for him to climb. When Gilbert and Marcus saw him making progress up the hill they began pelting him with snowballs made from the icy mound.

"Hey, cut it out," Charlie shouted, throwing his arms up to protect himself from the barrage. Then suddenly the school bell rang, sending children from all over the playground shouting and running for the double doors that led back inside where it was warm. Marcus tossed Charlie's *kufi* one last time to Gilbert, who flung it halfway across the school yard into a muddy slush puddle. Both Gilbert and Marcus slid down the bank of snow laughing and running toward the open school doors. Charlie followed close behind. Slipping and sliding in his sandals Charlie made his way over to the puddle where he fished his hat out. His beautiful rainbow-colored crown was filthy and soaking wet. And what was worse, Charlie was shivering all over now. And his toes were nearly frozen stiff.

5

Tamika and Ms. Potter were busy working on Tamika's festival dress when Charlie came home from school. The bronze-colored *lappa* dress that Tamika had chosen from the shop was much too long. So Tamika stood on a chair in front of the closet mirror and Ms. Potter knelt beside her. Carefully, with straight pins pressed between her lips, she placed the pins in a neat row exactly where Tamika's dress would later be hemmed. While her mother concentrated on her work Tamika busied herself by ad-

48

miring her own reflection in the mirror. On her head she wore a black velvet *kufi* sprinkled with tiny shimmering rhinestones. She did look pretty, if she must say so herself.

"Hold still so I can finish this now, Tamika," scolded Ms. Potter. "I've still got to get my supper started."

Scattered about the dining room table were an assortment of handmade Kwanzaa gifts for friends and relatives: a knit shawl for Mama Sarah who lived across the hall; for Ms. Cash in apartment 3-B, plant holders made from popsicle sticks; for the Jackson twins, a set of hand-carved wooden trucks; and for Uncle Jeb and Aunt Velma, a box of cowry shells and a wooden libation cup that Charlie and his father had carved together.

As Kwanzaa drew nearer the Potters' dining room table was beginning to look more like a *karamu* table. In the very center stood Charlie's rugged-looking *kinara*. Its red, black, and green candles were pressed solemnly into holes that had not all been carved to precision. For that reason, some of the candles, which were all supposed to be the same height, were uneven.

On the face of the *kinara* were gashes and nicks where Charlie's unsure hand had faltered or where the carving tool had slipped. And where Charlie had intended to finish the wood with a shiny shellacking, instead, he had mistakenly used a dull varnish on his brush. The *kinara* was so crude looking that Charlie was surprised to see it sitting on the celebration table, and filled with candles at that. But seeing it there made Charlie feel good. He knew it meant that his family was proud of the work he had done.

It was warm and cozy inside the apartment. But Charlie still felt a chill in his bones from the playground. Just thinking about it made him shiver. Charlie sneezed, and that was when Ms. Potter and Tamika noticed him.

"Hey, young man," said Ms. Potter affectionately. "Where'd you come from? I didn't even hear you come in." Charlie responded with a loud, hacking cough.

"Cover your mouth," complained Tamika.

"Tamika, don't you get started," cautioned Ms. Potter. "How was school today, champ?" she asked, removing the straight pins from her mouth. "Sounds like you're trying to come down with something. Come over here and let Mama feel your forehead, honey."

As Charlie drew nearer Tamika noticed her brother's runny nose. Charlie sneezed again. "Mama, make him cover his mouth."

"Tamika!" shushed Ms. Potter as she lay her hands on Charlie's cheeks and forehead. "You feel kind of warm," said his mother. Charlie wiped his nose with his hand.

"Mama make him — "

"Tamika, what did I tell you to do?" scolded Ms. Potter in a very serious tone.

Then Charlie jumped in, "I'm all right, Mama," he claimed.

"I think I'd better make you a cup of hot tea."

Ms. Potter pinned the last straight pin into the hem of Tamika's *lappa*. Then she turned to Charlie who was sitting on the couch and said, "Charlie Potter, what's taking you so long to get those boots off?" Before he could answer she got up from the floor. "Soon as you get those boots off you head straight for the kitchen, you hear?"

"Aw Mama," said Charlie.

"Aw Mama, nothing," said Ms. Potter, making her way into the kitchen.

But as soon as Ms. Potter left, Charlie got up and flopped himself down in a chair at the dining room table. He ran his hands across the gashes and nicks in his hand-carved *kinara*. He tried pressing the candles that looked too tall, deeper down inside the uneven holes. And the candles that looked too short, he tried to pull further out. He sat quietly rearranging the candles when suddenly the door to the apartment opened and he heard his father's booming voice.

"Hey, man!"

Charlie looked up to see his father walking through the door with a bag of groceries in each arm. A light dusting of snowflakes on the crown of Mr. Potter's ski cap and on the shoulders of his coat told Charlie that it was still snowing outside. Mr. Potter sniffed at the aroma of crisp fried chicken floating in the air. "Uummph! Something sure smells good in here," he said, closing the door behind him with the back of his foot. "I guess I don't have to ask you where your mama is." Then, without waiting for Charlie to answer, he winked at him and followed the aroma of supper into the kitchen.

When Mr. Potter returned Charlie was sitting on the sofa in his shirtsleeves struggling with his boots. In the struggle Charlie's school bag spilled to the floor, and out of the bag tumbled the muddy *kufi*. His grandfather's *kufi*, which had been handed down to him the year before. The one Gilbert and Marcus had played Frisbee with at lunch hour that afternoon. Only the hat no longer looked like a rainbow-colored *kufi* at all. Instead it was filthy and crushed, hardly recognizable.

"What happened to your *kufi*, son?" Mr. Potter asked, picking it up. "How'd it get so dirty and crushed?" Mr. Potter tried to straighten it out. But Charlie only shrugged. Too embarrassed to look up, Charlie stared at the floor. Mr. Potter knelt down beside his son. He paused for a moment, as though he were thinking about something. And then, with the *kufi* in his hand he asked, "How's our friend Gilbert been doing lately?"

Reluctantly Charlie looked at his father. "Not too good, Dad," he said.

Mr. Potter put the *kufi* down and cradled Charlie's face with both hands. Then the next thing Charlie knew, his father was putting his coat back on.

"Grab your coat, too, Charlie," he said.

"What's up, Dad?"

"Just come with me. I've got something I want to show you."

Just then Ms. Potter came from the kitchen with a cup of hot lemon tea. She put the teacup and saucer down on the table.

"Just where do you think you're running off to, Charlie Potter?" she asked good-naturedly but serious, too. Charlie covered his mouth and coughed, then zipped his jacket.

"With Dad," he said, trying to stifle another cough.

"Staying in the warm house wouldn't hurt that cold one bit," protested Ms. Potter. Mr. Potter took his ski cap off and put it on Charlie's head. Then he unwrapped his wool scarf from around his neck and tied it around his son's neck.

"I'll keep him warm," promised Mr. Potter. "There's something I need for the boy to see."

56

Downstairs, outside on the cold street, Charlie climbed inside his dad's old pick-up truck. As he sat beside his father in the passenger seat, Charlie wondered what was going on. Mr. Potter put the key in the ignition and revved the motor. Then he turned on his headlights and pointed the truck first toward California Avenue and then on toward Madison Street.

The ride down Madison Street was silent but the sights were familiar. They rode past the Shine King, where sometimes late on Saturday afternoons Mr. Potter sat and talked politics, or sports, with Red and Hops and Herbie. Or with Mr. Coleman, if Mr. Coleman wasn't too busy shining shoes. And sometimes his father would even have his shoes repaired, or spit shined so bright he could see his face reflected in them.

They rode past Jay Jay's fish market, where on Fridays Ms. Potter bought fresh fish, and past Edna's Soul Food Kitchen and Moon's Restaurant on the corner of

Madison and Western. As they neared the secondhand shop where used clothes and giant inflated toys hung in the window, Charlie kept his eye out for the used train set he'd had his heart set on for months now. Finally they reached the stadium, where a red traffic light stopped them.

Outside, on the streets, it was beginning to turn dark. Snow was still falling ever so lightly now. People were getting off buses coming from downtown, arriving home from work, and rushing to get out of the cold to warm suppers. Through the windows of the truck Charlie stared up at the purple night sky. The stars were all aglitter. On the street, lamp lights flickered off and on. Until finally they flickered on. Bright and strong. Flooding the streets in a soft pool of orange light. Charlie could hear his stomach growling. He was starting to get hungry for his supper.

When the traffic light turned green Mr. Potter rounded the corner and drove two more blocks. To Charlie's surprise, his father pulled into the parking lot of the Henry Horner housing projects, then turned off the ignition and car lights.

"Where we going, Dad?" Charlie asked nervously. From his friends, Charlie had heard bad things about the projects. There were gangs there that sometimes hurt people or robbed them.

"You don't have to be afraid, son," said Mr. Potter, peering out the front window of the truck. Then he pointed to one of the taller of the nineteen sky-scraping buildings that stood before them like giant gray soldiers saluting the darkness. "You see that building?" Charlie looked up to where his dad was pointing.

"The one with the blinking star on top?" asked Charlie. He glanced fretfully aroun the empty lot where they were parked.

"That's the one." For a moment his father was quiet. Finally he said, "That's where your Uncle Jeb, and I, and your Aunt Velma, and your Aunt Louise all grew up." Charlie stared blankly at the building. He

59

knew his father had grown up in the projects but they'd never really talked about it much. The Potters often passed by the "Hornets" on their way downtown, but Mr. Potter had never taken Charlie there before. Maybe it was because the people Mr. Potter had grown up with had all moved away from the "Hornets," just like Mr. Potter had done, a long, long time ago.

"I used to play sandlot in that baseball field," he said, pointing to a dark stretch of emptiness in the distance. "In the summertime anyway," he explained. "Winters, we'd all get together and flood the field. Then we'd play hockey or just ice skate."

Mr. Potter pressed his forehead against the windshield. "Look all the way up," he said to Charlie. "Just beneath the star on the top story. That's the thirteenth floor. That's where we lived. Your Aunt Velma used to call it the penthouse." Mr. Potter shook his head and laughed at the memories.

"The penthouse?" said Charlie, puzzled.

Then he blurted out, "Weren't you ashamed of living here?" But as soon as he'd said it, Charlie's own cheeks burned with shame. He hung his head. He'd just hurt his father's feelings and was at once sorry for what he'd said.

"Sorry, Dad," whispered Charlie.

Mr. Potter reached out and put his arm around Charlie's shoulder. He pulled him close to him.

"That's all right, champ," said Mr. Potter understandingly. "I think I know what you mean." Mr. Potter was quiet for a moment. And then he tried to explain things to Charlie. "There was nothing to be ashamed of, son," he said. "We had good times here. Good times."

Charlie scanned the dimly lit playground. Good times, he thought to himself. Shuh! Charlie saw nothing but a broken down old jungle gym. Broken seesaws. And no seats at all in any of the swings.

"I know what you're thinking," said Mr. Potter, looking out over the shabby, dimly lit buildings. "It wasn't always like this. I tell you when I was a kid, we practiced the Kwanzaa principle of *ujima* by hosing down that baseball diamond come winter. *Ujima* means to make life better. And that's what we did. It might not sound like much, but it sure meant a lot to us. It gave us something to do. Something that was fun. Instead of sitting around worrying all the time about being poor. Soon as the field turned to ice we'd skate and play hockey almost 'til spring. I still remember my first pair of ice skates. Your grandma bought them for me from the secondhand shop, right back down there on Madison Street. They were a pair of white figure skates. A pair of girl's skates."

"Girl's skates!" cried Charlie.

"That's right," Mr. Potter laughed. "If it weren't for your Uncle Jeb I would've gotten laughed right off the ice. It was your Uncle Jeb who turned those skates into boy's skates by polishing them black."

"Whew!" Charlie whistled a sigh of relief.

" 'Whew!' is right," agreed Mr. Potter, smiling. With thoughts of good times from his childhood lighting up his eyes he said, "I remember we used to get us a couple of milk crates to use for goalie nets, and for hockey sticks we used Mama's old broomsticks."

"Man, Daddy," teased Charlie, "y'all *was* poor."

Mr. Potter laughed softly to himself. Looking up at the thirteenth floor, he had to admit, "I guess we were, son. Only we didn't spend a lot of time thinking about it."

From out of the darkness of the high-rise dwellings two teenaged boys suddenly appeared. From a distance, it looked to Charlie as though the two boys were heading straight for his dad and him. Charlie could feel every muscle in his body tense up. The teens walked straight toward the truck, but as soon as they reached the edge of the baseball field where Charlie and his father were parked, the boys made a sharp turn and headed toward the bright lights and the twenty-four-hour grocery stores that dotted west Madison Street. Following them with his eyes, Charlie breathed a deep sigh of relief.

Mr. Potter, still looking up at his childhood home said, "Nope. We weren't rich. Nobody around here was rich. But we all practiced *umoja*. We helped each other out. Me, and your Aunt Velma, and your Uncle Jeb, and your Aunt Louise — we didn't have the best of clothes. But we were always clean. My mama saw to that. Grandma and Granddad worked long and hard. And it wasn't long before they'd saved enough money to get us out of the projects." Mr. Potter took Charlie by the chin and said, "Now does that sound like something to be embarrassed about?" Charlie shook his head no.

It started snowing more heavily and the wind picked up. It blew ghostlike drifts of snow across Mr. Potter's boyhood playing field. Charlie looked at his father and then out the window at the night sky. The blinking star above the thirteenth floor where his father and uncle and aunts had grown up seemed somehow brighter now.

"Buying a home was Grandma and Grandpa's purpose in life," Mr. Potter continued. "Their *nia*. That's all they ever talked about. Getting out of the projects and buying their own little house. Then after I grew up and got married, and you and Tamika came along, your grandma and grandpa put their house up, to help me raise money to open my own store."

"That's *ujamma*, Daddy," Charlie jumped in. "*Ujamma* means we build and support our own businesses."

"That's right, son," said Mr. Potter smiling proudly.

A woman walked past Charlie's side of the truck holding the hand of a boy about the same age as Charlie. The boy wore a school bag on his back just like the one Charlie owned. It made Charlie think of school. He thought about Gilbert and Marcus and how he was letting them ruin his holiday. He thought about the school Kwanzaa Festival, and about how much Kwanzaa had always meant to him, before Gilbert Crenshaw had come into the picture.

Outside the snow was beginning to stick. The flakes were forming soft wet layers on the hood of the truck.

"I don't know about you, son, but I'm getting cold," said Mr. Potter, turning the collar up on his jacket. "How's about we go see what your mama's got warming on the stove?" He turned the key in the ignition and fired up the engine. For some reason though, Charlie didn't feel cold. Not one bit. Instead, he felt something deep inside of him beginning to warm up again.

6

Dressed in a bright red Santa suit, a whiskered old man clanged his hollow bell at a bucket half filled with change on the corner of Madison and Whipple streets. Charlie and Louie raced past the red blur. They were on their way to the secondhand shop. When they reached the storefront, they stood outside marveling at the brightly colored toys on the other side of the window.

There were colored blocks. The kind Charlie had played with back in kindergarten. Gold wrapping paper, puzzles, and bead mazes sat beside an art box and easel. And in the center of the display stood a red Radio Flyer, trucks, and a sled, surrounded by a miniature Lionel train set. Wooden toy soldiers and red and white candy canes as tall as Charlie stood erect, saluting teddy bears. And baby dolls sat patiently in little brown rocking chairs.

Charlie fixed his eye on the miniature train set slowly chugging its way around a clay mountaintop. The train and track were so small they could both fit inside a suitcase. The train came with a caboose and seven cars, and the engine had a real head-light and whistle and real smoke that rose from its stack in a white cloud. Along the circle of track, tiny Scotch pine trees had been planted. There were two tunnels and a bridge over which the train could pass. And the mountains were snowcapped. Right beside the train stood two manne-quins dressed in secondhand Silver Surfer jackets.

"Oh, man!" exclaimed Louie, covering both ears with his hands. "That Silver Surfer is so cool, Charlie. Check it out." Charlie pressed his nose against the window. "Look at it, man," Louie said. "The shiny black one. With the gold trim." The Silver Surfer jacket that Louie had picked out hung from the shoulders of a mannequin about the same size as he was. There were silver buckles on the shoulders and on both sides of the waist. The wrists were trimmed in a bright gold embroidery. The jacket had a thick pile lining. An oversized hood. And down the right arm, in huge cursive letters, ran the words: *Silver Surfer*.

"That *is* awesome," Charlie agreed.

"Man, if I had one wish for Christmas, it would be for that Silver Surfer," said Louie wistfully. He was shivering now and his cheeks and ears were beginning to turn red.

Puzzled, Charlie stared at his friend. Charlie had never thought about asking for clothes for Kwanzaa, although to his dis-

appointment he had often gotten them anyway. Not a Kwanzaa went by that he didn't receive underwear and socks from Aunt Joanie or Aunt Velma. Or maybe even a knitted sweater from Grandma. But the longer he stood there looking at Louie freezing in his baseball jacket in the middle of winter, the better he began to understand why Louie might wish for a jacket for a Christmas present, instead of toys.

He put his arm around Louie's shoulders. "It's freezing out here, man," he said. "Let's go in."

The warmth inside the shop slowly melted the red from Louie's cheeks and ears. The owner of the shop took the Silver Surfer jacket from the window and let Louie try it on. He let Charlie work the switches on the train set.

Charlie maneuvered the train over the tiny tracks with precision. The train slowly climbed the tracks along the mountainsides and Charlie made it whistle when it reached the bridge's overpass. When it slowed in the depot to pick up passengers, Charlie let fly the whistle again. Each time it reached the tunnels, Charlie would turn on the engine's headlight and flood the dark passageways in a pool of bright yellow beams. Again and again Charlie maneuvered the train through its paces. From mountaintop to depot. Over bridges and through tunnels. He had become completely lost in the train ride until Louie elbowed him out of his reverie.

"Man," said Louie, reading Charlie's mind, "that *is* a nice train. You've been saving up forever, Charlie. When are you going to buy it?"

"Been wanting me another train for a long time now," answered Charlie. He picked up a freight car and examined the shiny metal wheels. "The wheels on my cars are all busted up."

"I'll even help you carry the pennies to the shop," offered Louie. Charlie smiled. He held up his right hand and the two boys delivered a high five to each other. Then he turned to put the freight car back in the display.

"It's beginning to get dark outside," Louie said, turning up the collar to his jacket. "We better get out of here." Outside the window of the toy shop Charlie could see people leaning against the gale wind as they pushed their way down the street. Some were tightening the woolen scarves around their necks. A man wearing a ski mask with slits for eyes and nose was frantically pulling the mask from around the top of his head to down over his face and chin. And in front of the shop, the branches of an elm were waving furiously in the strong gusts.

Charlie glanced at Louie. Realizing he would freeze to death walking home in his thin jacket, Charlie unzipped his own jacket. He took it off. Then he took off the hooded sweatshirt he was wearing underneath. He handed the sweatshirt to Louie. "Here," he offered, "you might need this."

Sheepishly, Louie accepted the sweat-shirt from his friend. "Hey thanks a lot, Charlie," he said. As Louie dressed, Charlie put his jacket and cap back on. Louie pulled the sweatshirt hood over his head and then tied the string tightly underneath his chin. Together they walked to the door of the shop where Charlie placed his hand on the warm knob.

"Ready, soldier?" he asked.

"Ready!" Louie answered. Charlie snatched the door wide open. Then the two boys ran down Madison Street all the way home, as though their very lives depended on it.

7

"This is dumb!" said Gilbert.

"Gilbert, stand still!" said Ms. Marmelsteen, sounding annoyed. Ms. Marmelsteen wrestled a black *dashiki* over Gilbert's shoulders and then she topped it off by placing a matching *kufi* on his head. Since Gilbert had been chosen to greet parents for the Kwanzaa Festival, he had had to don an African costume, and he was not happy about it. Fully dressed now, Gilbert kept fidgeting. He looked as though he were trying to work himself out of his costume.

"Gilbert, you really must try and cooperate!" said Ms. Marmelsteen, her patience wearing thin. "I really can't quite imagine what's come over you. Why a person would think you were *dying* to play an important role in our festival, what with all the classroom participation you've contributed. This is your moment to shine, Gilbert," sang Ms. Marmelsteen, throwing both her hands in the air. "This is your big chance!"

A wave of laughter rose and the children threatened to explode until Ms. Marmelsteen clapped her hands sharply. As she was quieting the class Mr. Dinwiddie, the school janitor, stepped into the room. Mr. Dinwiddie was short and stout with dark whiskers and a bushy mustache.

"Ms. Marmelsteen, all five of your booths are set up," smiled the toothless janitor.

"All five!" cried Ms. Marmelsteen nervously.

"All five," repeated Mr. Dinwiddie, showing his pink gums.

"Mr. Dinwiddie!" exclaimed Ms. Marmelsteen, upset. "There should be *nine* booths, not *five* booths!"

"Nine? Dang gummit!" said Mr. Dinwiddie, scratching his head. "I could've swore — "

"Mr. Dinwiddie! How could you!" cried Ms. Marmelsteen running past the janitor, across the hall and into the gymnasium. "Children!" she shouted over her shoulder to the fidgety fourth-graders, "be still! Please!" But as soon as Ms. Marmelsteen disappeared a wave of laughter flooded the room. Everyone was laughing now except for Gilbert who had a huge frown plastered all over his face. With Ms. Marmelsteen gone, Gilbert snatched the *kufi* from his head. And then, for no apparent reason, he stormed straight over to where Louie sat.

"What're you laughing at?" barked Gilbert.

"Nothing, man. I wasn't laughing at you," said Louie. "I wasn't even looking at — " Before Louie could finish his sentence Gilbert had lifted Louie out of his seat by his shirt collar.

"Hey, what's the matter with you?" Louie shrieked. "Get your hands off me, *estupido*."

"Stupid? Who you calling stupid you little — "

"Why don't you pick on somebody your own size?" a voice said. Then before Gilbert knew it, he was standing toe to toe with Charlie Potter.

Gilbert let go of Louie's shirt and faced off with Charlie. "Who's gonna make me?" he threatened.

"Nobody," answered Charlie.

"Nobody?" laughed Gilbert. He glanced around the classroom trying to gather support. "Hey, listen to this moron everybody. First he jumps into somebody else's fight and next he says nobody's gonna do nothing about it. What a weenie," he clucked. A nervous laughter rose in the classroom and then just as quickly died down.

"Nobody's going to do anything to anybody," said Charlie. Gilbert drew closer to Charlie until their noses were practically touching. The two boys stared each other down. Gilbert clenched his fists. Charlie didn't want to fight, but he wasn't going to back down either. He glanced nonchalantly at Gilbert's clenched fists.

"Fighting won't prove anything," said Charlie. "You're just mad because Ms. Marmelsteen is making you be in the Kwanzaa Festival and you're trying to take it out on everybody else."

"Says who, chicken breath," smirked Gilbert, breathing hard in Charlie's face.

"Me," said Charlie, standing his ground. "If you knew what Kwanzaa was all about you wouldn't be acting this way."

"Oh? What's it all about?" Gilbert whined, trying to draw Charlie into a fight. "African clothes and goofy hats?" Gilbert laughed, clutching his stomach and making a spectacle of himself. But nobody, not one person in class, laughed.

"No, it's not about that," said Charlie. "It's about helping other people, and making life better, and standing up for what's right and doing the right thing."

"Tell him, Charlie," said Louie, backing up his best friend.

"Yeah, Charlie, you tell him," chimed in three other boys from the front of the class. The sound of desks and chairs scraping the floor made Gilbert glance around. One by one everybody stood up. Before he knew it, the whole class had formed into a crowd behind Charlie. Gilbert's face turned red as he soon realized that no one was on his side.

"Oh, so now I'm wrong and you're right," said Gilbert, getting mad all over again. "I'm getting pretty sick of you and your smart mouth."

"Listen, Gilbert," said Charlie calmly, "Kwanzaa is a holiday of lights, and I'm not going to let you change that."

"Boys!" Ms. Marmelsteen's shrill voice suddenly interrupted. "Charlie! Gilbert! What's going on here?" Facing Gilbert she said, "We'll have no more of your nonsense today, Gilbert! Class! Line up at the door immediately! The festival is about to begin." All that was left of Gilbert and Charlie's argument was the shuffling of feet, mixed in with the exhilarating expectation of no more class for the rest of the afternoon.

Ms. Marmelsteen planted an unhappy Gilbert at the gymnasium door, where already parents had begun to gather, before taking the rest of the class inside for the festival. Once inside, each member of the class had a booth to attend or game stations where traditional African games were to be played with visitors. Red, black, and green streamers were hung wall-to-wall along with red, black, and green balloons, which decorated the basketball rims.

In the back of the hall, Charlie could see his mother and father putting some last-minute finishing touches on their booth. Draped across the front of their booth were dazzling strips of colorful *kente* cloth and

bright, bold *dashiki* shirts and *kufi* crowns. Charlie's mother and father were decked out in matching suits.

The smell of fou fou, barbecued chicken, and couscous filled the air. And on stage was the most beautiful Kwanzaa *karamu* feast table that Charlie had ever seen. Bowls, brimming over with grapes, pomegranates, oranges, and cassavas sat at both ends. And in the center of the celebration table was the wooden *kinara* that Charlie had made. He had decided to make his *kinara* a Kwanzaa present to his fourth-grade class.

When it was almost three o'clock and time for school to let out, Ms. Marmelsteen set up the slide projector and dimmed the gymnasium lights. On stage with his father, Charlie stood behind the Kwanzaa candles in front of the crowd of parents, students, and teachers gathered around. As he lit each candle in honor of Kwanzaa, Charlie recited the seven Kwanzaa principles into the microphone.

"*Umoja* means we help each other."

"*Umoja*," repeated the crowd.

"*Kujichagulia* means we decide things for ourselves."

"*Kujichagulia*," the chorus sang out loud.

"*Ujima* means we work together to make life better."

"*Ujima*."

"*Ujamma* means we build and support our own businesses."

"*Ujamma*."

"*Nia* means we have a reason for living."

"*Nia*," came back the resound.

"*Kuumba* means we use our minds and hands to make things."

"*Kuumba*."

"*Imani* means we believe in ourselves and in our ancestors."

"*Imani*," shouted the crowd.

And then, as loud as he could, Charlie shouted too. "Happy Kwanzaa, everybody!"

"Happy Kwanzaa!" shouted the festival goers. At the top of their lungs.

8

One week later, at sunset, the door of the Potter apartment was left wide open. The smell of fried chicken, mustard and turnip greens, cornbread and candied yams floated out into the hallway and underneath the doors of all the other apartments. Charlie was starved. That was the hardest thing about waiting for the *karamu* feast. From sunrise to sunset on the sixth day of Kwanzaa his family and friends did not eat. At the end of the day, everyone gathered together for the *karamu*.

Before long the doors to the other apartments opened and neighbors began to pour out into the hall. Some carried huge bowls and platters filled with the smell of delicious things to eat. Ms. Cash from apartment 3B had cooked the biggest roast turkey Charlie had ever seen. And from across the hall, Mama Sarah brought a pot of steaming hot jambalaya and a three-tiered coconut-pineapple cake.

By the time Louie arrived with Charlie's favorite, a bowl of rice and spicy beans, the Potter apartment was filled to the rafters with neighbors, relatives, and friends. Grandpa and Grandma Potter, Aunt Joanie, Aunt Velma and Uncle Jeb couldn't get over how big Charlie was getting.

As Louie walked out of the Potter kitchen Charlie beckoned to his friend. "Hey, Louie," he called, "come this way. Got something I want you to see." He grabbed Louie's arm and together they made a bee-line for his room.

Once inside Charlie crawled under his

bed where he found his plastic penny jug. He pulled the jug out and emptied the pennies into a tall tin cookie can. Then he walked over to Louie and handed the heavy canister to him. Charlie smiled. "Happy Kwanzaa," he said.

"Happy Kwanzaa?" said Louie, surprised. "What's up, Charlie?" he asked, stumbling under the heavy weight of the can. "I thought these pennies were for your train set."

"*Was* for my train set. Anyhow," he shrugged it off, "I've had my eye on something else."

"Something else?" said Louie. "Something else like what? You've been saving up forever to buy the train."

Charlie walked over to his desk and picked up his old caboose and a couple of freight cars. He ran his fingers across the lifeless wheels. Then he turned to face his friend.

"Saw me this *awesome* black jacket with the *coolest* gold trim in the secondhand shop," he said. "Thick pile lining. Oversized hood. And the words *Silver Surfer* — " Charlie stopped. He made eye contact with Louie. "Had the name 'Louie' written all over it."

Louie was speechless. He put the pennies down clumsily on the floor. "Gee Charlie," he murmured. "I don't know what to say." Charlie walked up to him. He put his hand on Louie's shoulder. The two boys stood quietly staring at the can.

"Just say we're friends," said Charlie.

They looked up at each other and frowned. Then they smiled their crooked smiles and broke out in laughter. It was a hearty laughter that told them they would always be best friends. Charlie put his arm around Louie's shoulder. "Let's go eat," he said. "It's almost time for the *karamu* to begin."

It was sunset now. Ms. Potter dimmed the lights in the living room and one by one the crowd grew quiet and gathered around the table.

"Harambee!" greeted Ms. Potter.

"Harambee!" everyone answered.

She welcomed everyone to the Kwanzaa celebration and to the *karamu* feast. Then she leaned over the *kinara* and lit the candle in the center, a black one for *umoja* or unity. Then she lit a red candle. Then next a green one. She kept on lighting candles until five of the seven glowed warmly on the faces of the people gathered around the dimly lit room. She beckoned to Charlie to come to the table to light a red candle for the sixth celebration day.

When he reached the table Ms. Potter handed him the flame. Charlie looked around the room. Even with the Christmas lights blinking in the front room window he could barely make out the faces of the crowd sitting back in the semidarkness. But he could make out Louie's face sitting on the sofa next to Mama Sarah. Louie was clutching the can of pennies in his lap and waving and smiling at Charlie. Charlie smiled back at him, and then he lit the red

Kwanzaa candle. Lighting the candle made Charlie feel all grown up.

"Today," he said, "I light a red candle for *kuumba*."

"*Kuumba* . . ." repeated the roomful of neighbors and friends.

"*Kuumba* means creativity," said Charlie. "It means we must use our minds and our hands to make things. And our hearts, too," he added. "In good times and bad."

Out of the corner of his eye Charlie saw Tamika standing with their father. He suddenly realized how pretty Tamika looked in the velvet and rhinestone crown she wore and in the *lappa* that she and their mother had worked so hard on. He thought about his father, and how, as a little boy, he had used *kuumba* to play hockey on the winter baseball fields in Henry Horner projects, using milk crates and broomsticks. And how he himself had used *kuumba* to try to get Gilbert to see what Kwanzaa was really all about. Charlie smiled. But this time the smile wasn't just

for his best friend Louie. This time it was meant for everyone.

Later that night, after everyone had gone home and Mr. and Ms. Potter had finished the dishes, Mr. Potter found Charlie in his bedroom counting a handful of pennies. Mr. Potter picked up the empty jug and held it up to the ceiling light.

"What happened to all your pennies, man?"

Charlie shrugged his shoulders.

"Well now, something happened to them," insisted Mr. Potter.

Finally Charlie said, "Mr. Rodriguez lost his job at Thanksgiving."

"That's too bad," said Mr. Potter sympathetically.

"I gave my pennies to Louie for a Kwanzaa present. He needed a winter jacket really bad."

Mr. Potter was quiet for a moment and then he said, "That was really thoughtful of you, Charlie."

"I guess," said Charlie, shrugging his

shoulders again. Mr. Potter fished for some change in his pocket and then handed the coins to Charlie. "Thanks, Dad," said Charlie. He dropped the coins one by one into his plastic penny jug.

"I've got something else for you," Mr. Potter said after a long pause. Then he turned to leave. When he returned, Mr. Potter carried a gift-wrapped box. He handed the gift to Charlie. The box was not that neatly wrapped. Not like when Ms. Potter wrapped presents. Charlie could tell that his father had wrapped it. And that it had been done just now, in a hurry.

"What is it?" asked Charlie, shaking the box near his ear.

"Open it and see," his father teased. Charlie tore the wrapping from the box.

"I was saving this for your twelfth birthday," said Mr. Potter sincerely. "But from what I can tell, you've already earned it."

Inside the box Charlie found a brightly colored *kente* cloth, just like the one that belonged to his Uncle Jeb and his father.

There were patches of yellow at both ends followed by black patches, red, green, orange, blue, and gold. And there was a matching *kufi* to wear with it.

"The yellow stands for good luck," explained his father. Green stands for prosperity. Blue means happiness. And gold — "

"Gold is for royalty," Charlie finished, "we learned that in class."

Charlie stood in front of the mirror and tried on his crown. He put the *kente* strip around his neck, and then he smiled at what he saw.

"Thanks, Dad," he said, giving his father a long hug.

Later that night, when Mr. Potter went to tuck Charlie in, he found beneath the quilt Charlie's *kente* cloth, still draped around his neck, and his new *kufi* still on his head.

9

After midnight, later that night, Grandma Potter had lit the last Kwanzaa candle. Charlie had tried to stay awake, but no matter how hard he tried he could not fight sleep. In the morning, sunlight had crept on kitten paws through Charlie's bedroom window. Charlie got up and dressed. Then right after breakfast he went looking for his best friend. Maybe they would spend part of the day at the secondhand shop. Charlie wanted to see if the train set was still there.

"Hey Louie," he yelled up to the third floor flat of Louie's apartment building. But Louie didn't come to the window. Instead, Mr. Rodriguez came. He opened the window and stuck out his balding head.

"*Ay, niño*," yelled Mr. Rodriguez, waving at Charlie. "*Feliz Navidad* and a Happy New Year!"

"Happy Kwanzaa, Mr. Rodriguez, and Happy New Year to you too," Charlie yelled back. "Is Louie home? Can he come out?"

"*Sí, Sí*," smiled Mr. Rodriguez. "*Un momento.* One minute." Before he turned to go Mr. Rodriguez yelled down, "Hey Charlie! Thank you very much for giving Louie the Kwanzaa gift. Louie says, you helped make the *piñata*, too. It was *bee-yoo-ti-ful!*" Charlie waved at Mr. Rodriguez and smiled. Then Mr. Rodriguez's head disappeared inside the hole of the apartment window just as quickly as it had appeared.

It was starting to get cold now. So Charlie tied his *kente* strip around his neck like a muffler to keep himself warm. Finally Louie emerged from out of the dark hallway wearing his new Silver Surfer jacket and munching on a slice of wheat toast.

"Hey," said Louie, running his hand over Charlie's brightly colored *kente*. "Where'd you get that?"

"From my dad," Charlie smiled proudly. "It's a *kente* strip."

"Just like the one Ms. Marmelsteen showed in class," Louie remembered. "Pretty cool," he said.

The two friends started out walking. Before long, they broke out into a jog along California Avenue. They were heading toward Madison Street and the secondhand shop. High above their heads the cloud-filled sky slowly opened its mouth. A smattering of snowflakes began to fall, like down feathers, drifting softly to the ground. In front of the secondhand shop, both boys slid on the new snow to a halt.

"Hey, Charlie," Louie smiled, looking up at the sky. "It's beginning to look a lot like

Kwanzaa, don't you think?" Charlie looked up at the sky. He stuck his tongue out and let the icy snowflakes melt in his warm mouth.

"It sure is, Louie," he smiled. "It sure is."

About the Author

Debbi Chocolate is the author of numerous popular and award-winning books for young readers, including *Talk, Talk*, for which she received the Parents Choice Award; *On The Day I Was Born*, a Children's Book Council Notable selection; and *Neate to the Rescue!*

Ms. Chocolate lives with her husband and two sons in a suburb of Chicago.

LITTLE 🍎 APPLE®

Here are some of our favorite Little Apples.

Once you take a bite out of a Little Apple book—you'll want to read more!

Books for Kids with BIG Appetites!

- ☐ NA45899-X **Amber Brown Is Not a Crayon**
  Paula Danziger $2.99
- ☐ NA42833-0 **Catwings** Ursula K. LeGuin $3.50
- ☐ NA42832-2 **Catwings Return** Ursula K. LeGuin $3.50
- ☐ NA41821-1 **Class Clown** Johanna Hurwitz $3.50
- ☐ NA42400-9 **Five True Horse Stories** Margaret Davidson $3.50
- ☐ NA42401-7 **Five True Dog Stories** Margaret Davidson $3.50
- ☐ NA43868-9 **The Haunting of Grade Three**
  Grace Maccarone $3.50
- ☐ NA40966-2 **Rent a Third Grader** B.B. Hiller $3.50
- ☐ NA41944-7 **The Return of the Third Grade Ghost Hunters**
  Grace Maccarone $2.99
- ☐ NA47463-4 **Second Grade Friends** Miriam Cohen $3.50
- ☐ NA45729-2 **Striped Ice Cream** Joan M. Lexau $3.50

Available wherever you buy books...or use the coupon below.

- -

SCHOLASTIC INC., P.O. Box 7502, 2931 East McCarty Street, Jefferson City, MO 65102

Please send me the books I have checked above. I am enclosing $ _____ (please add $2.00 to cover shipping and handling). Send check or money order—no cash or C.O.D.s please.

Name_____

Address_____

City_____State/Zip_____

Please allow four to six weeks for delivery. Offer good in the U.S.A. only. Sorry, mail orders are not available to residents of Canada. Prices subject to change.

LAP198